Barbie™

Awesome Parties

Written by Debra Mostow Zakarin

Illustrated by Joann Owen Coy

Art Direction and Design by Allison Higa
Photography of Models by James Atiee, Susan Kurtz, Rhonda Snyder, Lisa Collins, and Judy Tsuno
Photography of Barbie Skirt Cake by Bill Kroll, Sheryl Tetrick, Leila May, and Judy Tsuno
Photography of Other Products by Eye Four Color, Marina del Rey, California
Creation and Styling of Crafts and Edible Products by Allison Higa

Party favors provided courtesy of Tara Toy Corporation.
Barbie party goods are available where Party Express products are sold. Call 1-800-371-1288.
Use of Barbie Tea Party Serving Set provided courtesy of ARCOTOYS, INC., a Mattel company.

A Golden Book • New York
Golden Books Publishing Company, Inc.
New York, New York 10106

Use this list to plan every party!

Barbie's Party Countdown Checklist:

- ♡ Get parents' OK for a party
- ♡ Figure out where it will take place
- ♡ Decide on the number of guests and make a list
- ♡ Figure out how much money you can spend
- ♡ Pick the date
- ♡ Call your best friend and let her or him know

6 weeks to go
- ♡ Make party invitations
- ♡ Hand out or mail the invitations

2 weeks to go
- ♡ Buy or make party favors, decorations, and prizes
- ♡ Buy paper plates, cups, napkins, and balloons
- ♡ Make a list of games you will play
- ♡ Choose the music
- ♡ Choose party clothes or make a party costume

1 week to go
- ♡ Buy nonperishable ingredients for the food

2 days to go
- ♡ Baking day: Bake the cookies, cake, and any food that needs to go into the fridge
- ♡ Buy all the perishable food items

1 day to go
- ♡ Decorate your party room or backyard
- ♡ Wrap up the party favors

8 hours to go
- ♡ Set the table
- ♡ Make the fresh food and drinks
- ♡ Set out and prepare all the games

3 hours to go
- ♡ Blow up the balloons
- ♡ Take a shower and get dressed

1 hour to go
- ♡ Put out the food
- ♡ Check party room: Is everything ready?
- ♡ Sit down with a glass of lemonade and relax!

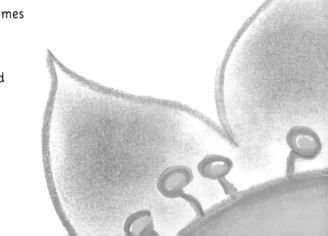

Dear Friend,

AWESOME PARTIES will help you plan some really cool and fun parties! This book is full of invitation ideas, easy crafts activities, games, and tons of recipes for everything you need to host the perfect party! For added fun, feel free to mix and match the game, craft, and recipe ideas from different party themes in this book.

 Whenever you see this sign, it means that you need to have a parent or other adult help you with the craft or recipe. Don't take any chances with safety! Always have an adult around to help when you see this sign!

And remember, you don't need tons of money or lots of people to have a great bash. With just the right amount of planning, a few munchies, a little imagination, and some good friends, you can throw the ultimate in cool, Barbie-themed parties!

Have fun!

Love,

Barbie

Happy Birthday Circus Party

Don't wait for the circus to come
to you—create a birthday circus in
your own home! If you have a big backyard,
have the party outside. If not, try the basement,
family room, living room, bedroom, or playroom.
Parties are lots of fun and lots of work! But don't
feel like you have to do everything by yourself.
Ask your mom, dad, older siblings, and best
friend to help you make your party the best!

Barbie Party Hint:
Make a copy of Barbie's
Party Countdown Checklist
(p.2) and start using it
for each party!

It's a Party!
Where: Jill's house
333 Forest St.
When: Jan. 7
11:30 a.m.
RSVP: (880) 555-1212

Invitations: Bag It!

Be creative with your invitations.
Use paper lunch bags. On one side of the bag
draw some clowns, lollipops, elephants—even a girl
on a tightrope. On the other side, give all of the important details of
your party: your name, address, date and time of party, and phone
number for your friends to RSVP. Fill the bag with popcorn, peanuts,
and candy. Tape it shut, and then tie it with a ribbon. Since these
invitations are hard to mail, you can hand them out after school or
have a parent take you to your friends' homes.

Invitations: Don't Bag It!

If you don't have enough time to make and deliver bagged invitations, then try paper balloon invitations. Cut colored construction paper into the shape of a balloon, and write down all of the party information. These will be much easier to pop into an envelope and mail. If you're missing an address, your parents or the class president can probably help you track it down.

P.S. Parties are a good way to make new friends! And everybody likes to be included, so try to invite your whole class if you can.

Big Top Party Area

If you have a very large tent, put it up! But if your circus party is inside, you can still pretend that you're under a Big Top by dividing your party room into three circles. In each circle you can have a different activity or game going on at the same time. Make sure to decorate your Big Top party area with lots of colorful streamers and balloons.

Did you know that RSVP stands for *répondez s'il vous plaît* in French? It means "please reply!"

Buy the birthday cake at your favorite bakery or bake one with your best friend. Don't forget to include an extra candle for good luck!

Circus Games & Activities

Face Painting Activity

Buy some children's face paint. Spread everything out on a table on top of old newspapers. Two or more people at a time can go to the table and paint each other's faces. Have a contest to see whose face is the silliest or looks the most like a clown. Give the winner a mini-makeup kit or pocket mirror.

Pin the Nose on the Clown Game

Before the party begins, draw a picture of a clown without a nose on a large piece of paper. Tape it to the wall. Cut out enough round noses for each guest to have one with his or her name on it. Attach some double-stick tape to the back of each nose. Here's how to play: The players line up in front of the nose-less clown. One at a time the players are given a nose, blindfolded with a bandanna, spun around three times, and pointed in the direction of the clown. Each player tries to stick their paper nose in the right place. The player who comes the closest is the winner!

Walk the Tightrope Game

Have your guests pretend they are walking on a tightrope. If your party is outside, use some chalk to draw a long line on the pavement. If your party is inside, then put masking tape across the floor. Take turns "walking" the "tightrope." The person who walks the furthest without "falling off" is the winner. Wanna go for bust? Draw or tape down a zigzagging line!

Peanut Butter and Jelly (PB&J) Pinwheels

For pinwheels, you'll need:
* 2 slices of white bread
* peanut butter
* jelly

Spread some peanut butter on the first slice of bread. Place the second slice of bread on top and spread on some jelly. Next, roll the bread into the shape of a cylinder. Press it tight and slice. *Voilà!* Wheel-shaped sandwiches. Not everybody likes PB&J, so make sure that you have some other sandwich choices.

Visit your local party outlet or stationery store for some cool and inexpensive party favors!

Clown Cones

For each clown cone, you'll need:
* one scoop ice cream (any flavor)
* one sugar cone
* jelly beans
* red candies
* one small plate

Place one scoop of ice cream on a small plate. Top it with a sugar-cone hat. Next make a clown face by adding jelly bean eyes and a red candy mouth. Freeze until ready to serve. (Although this might use up all the room in your freezer, the cones stay on better if you put them on before freezing.)

Parting Party Bags

Give your guests a party-favor bag. Decorate paper bags with pictures of balloons and clowns. Fill them up with peanuts in the shell (just like you get at the circus), a bottle of blowing bubbles, and maybe even Polaroid snapshots of your friends, taken at the party, with their faces painted!

Heart-to-Heart Valentine's Day Party

Have-a-Heart Invitations

For this Valentine's Day celebration, begin by giving your friends a heart-shaped valentine invitation. On the outside of the invitation write: *Be My . . .* and on the inside write: *Valentine Guest*. Decorate the heart with stickers and gold glitter. Ask all of your guests to wear red to the party. If you are in a goofy mood the day of your party, draw a red heart on your cheek!

Be My . . .

Valentine Guest

Where:
Cindy's house
432 Maple Ave.
When: Feb. 14, 11:30 a.m.
RSVP: (880) 555-1212
Please wear red

Barbie Party Hint:
Take lots of pictures so that after your party you can create a Heart-to-Heart party album!

Hearty Decorations

Go crazy! Fill your party room with pink and red heart-shaped balloons. Cover the walls with different sized hearts, using textures besides paper, such as felt or even T-shirt material. Make sure that candy hearts and heart-shaped chocolates are on every table.

Hunting for Hearts Activity

Before your guests arrive, cut many different
colored pieces of paper into heart shapes.
Hide them in different places throughout
your party room. To play, each guest
must collect as many pairs of hearts
of the same color as he or she can.
The person with the most
matching pairs wins a prize.

Heartfelt Fun Activity

Before your party begins, fill a big clear jar with lots of heart-shaped
candies. Count the candies as you fill up the jar, and write down the
amount on a piece of paper so that you don't forget it. Put the piece of
paper in a safe place. When your guests arrive, have them write down
their name and how many candies they think are in the jar. The person
who guesses closest to the correct amount in the jar is the winner
and gets to take
home the
candy jar!

Prizes

You don't need to spend a lot of money on prizes, and they don't have to be very big. You can find some neat items at your local party outlet or stationery store, such as blowing bubbles, magnets, pencils, key chains, hair barrettes, and even pocket mirrors. Or, a few days before your party, try making heart-shaped award certificates that say your guest is a winner!

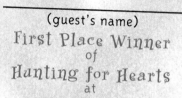

——————————
(guest's name)

First Place Winner
of
Hunting for Hearts
at
——————————'s
(your name)

Valentine
Party

The Ha, Ha, Ha Game

Ha, Ha, Ha is a great game to play with as few as two people, but the more the merrier! The object of the game is NOT to laugh. Sit in a circle. One player begins by saying, "Ha!" The person to the right continues with, "Ha, Ha!" The next follows with, "Ha, Ha, Ha!" and so on around the circle with each person adding another "Ha!" Each player must pronounce the "Ha!" as seriously as possible to avoid laughing as long as possible. Any player who laughs while "Ha-ing" or makes any mistake must drop out. However, he or she can still try to make the remaining players in the circle laugh—without touching or tickling them! The last person left in the circle is the winner.

Strawberry Ice Cream Sodas

For each soda, you'll need:
- 1 cup milk
- 1 cup seltzer
- 2 scoops strawberry ice cream

Mix the milk and seltzer together.
Add the ice cream. Yummmmy!

Heart-to-Heart Menu
Candy Hearts
Heart-Shaped Chocolates
Chicken Salad Sandwiches
Strawberry Ice Cream Sodas
Tuna Sandwiches
Sugar Cookies

Hearty Appetite

Serve up some tuna sandwiches.
Cut them into heart shapes
with a metal cookie cutter.
For dessert, gather everyone
together and make
strawberry ice cream
sodas. Then eat them
with heart-shaped
sugar cookies.

 ## Simply Delicious Sugar Cookies

To make 12–18 cookies, you'll need:
- 1 cup butter
- 1/2 cup white sugar
- 1/2 cup brown sugar
- 1 egg
- 1 teaspoon baking powder
- 1 teaspoon vanilla
- 3 cups flour
- 1/4 teaspoon salt
- red sugar crystals
- colored sprinkles
- heart-shaped cookie cutters

Preheat oven to 350° F. In a large bowl, mix all
of the ingredients together except red crystals
and sprinkles. With a rolling pin, flatten the
mixture until it is 1/4 inch thick. Then use the
cookie cutters to cut out the shapes. Decorate your
cookies with red sugar crystals and colored sprinkles.
On a greased cookie tray, space the cookies about
2 inches apart. Bake at 350° F for 12 minutes or until
the edges turn brown. Watch carefully so that the
cookies don't burn. Have an adult take them out of
the oven. Let cool in the pan for 20 minutes. Use a
spatula to lift from tray and place on a plate. Enjoy!

Thank-You-for-Coming Party Favors

For party favors, decorate red bags
with some heart-shaped stickers and fill
them up with soap (heart shaped, of course),
hair barrettes, and chocolate kisses.

Picnic Party

Picnic Setup

Before your guests arrive, set down a large blanket (or a bunch of smaller blankets or beach towels) to make a picnic area. Then place down the following items: snacks, picnic foods, paper plates, and paper napkins. Decorate with cute critter paperweights, which will also help to keep the paper napkins from blowing away if your picnic party is outside.

P Cute Critters Activity

A week or so before your party, decorate stones to look like cute bugs and use them as paperweights.
Materials needed:
• stones
• nontoxic paints
• varnish (spray or liquid)
• brushes
Collect stones of different sizes. Paint the stones to look like ants, ladybugs, or any other kind of six-legged creature. Have an adult help you give your rock paperweights a coat of clear varnish.

Outdoor Fun Games Hint

If it's not raining, organize some outdoor games. If there are boys and girls at your party, try to have an equal number of boys and girls on each team.

Peanut Race Game

It's best to hold this race on carpet or on grass. Each player is given a peanut in the shell. He or she lines up behind the starting line on hands and knees. Make the finish line about ten feet away. The first player to push the peanut to the finish line with his or her nose wins!

Potato Chips
Corn Chips
Bean or Salsa Chip Dip
Cold Barbecued Chicken
Potato Salad
Fruit Salad
Bug Juice

Picnic Barbecue

Every picnic needs to have some cold barbecued chicken and potato salad. The morning of the party would be the best time to barbecue the chicken with an adult. But don't forget the bug juice to wash it all down. What's bug juice? Fruit punch!

Red Rover, Red Rover Outdoor Game

Form two equal teams with one captain each and at least five players. Each team lines up facing each other, with the largest possible area between the teams. Team #1, standing in a line, holds hands, and their captain calls a member from the other team over by calling out, "Red rover, red rover, send _____ (name of a player on the other team) right over." The player from Team #2 who was called runs over and tries to break through the line of hands. If he or she is successful, then a member of the team whose line was broken through must be sent over to the opposing team. If he or she is unsuccessful, that player must join the team he or she just tried to break through. Now it is the other team's turn to line up holding hands and to call someone over to their side. The team with the most players after 10 rounds, wins.

Barbie Party Hint:
Be prepared for a mess and have plenty of garbage bags handy.

Crab Relay Outdoor Game

Divide your guests up into two teams. If there is an odd number of people, take turns being the referee or cheering squad for both teams. Make a starting line on one side of the yard, and a finish line on the other side of the yard. Line up both teams behind the starting line. At a signal from the referee, the first player of each team crawls backward on all fours from the starting line. Once their arms cross the finish line, they can stand up and run back to the start. At the starting line, they tag their next team member crawler in line, who sets off backward toward the finish line. The first team to have every player return to the start, wins!

So Long Party Favors

As a parting gift to your guests, fill a small bag with peanuts in their shells, gummy bears, and one of your cute stone critters!

Super Sleepover Party

Pajama Party!

Sleeping bags take up a lot of room, so before you invite your friends, figure out the best room to hold your party. It's great if the party room also has a bathroom nearby so that your friends won't have to wander around in the dark in the middle of the night.

Sleepover Party Invitations

Give your friends invitations cut in the shape of pajamas or a nightgown and ask them to arrive at your party in their pj's and robe! Be sure to ask them to bring along a sleeping bag, toothbrush, and clothes for the next morning!

Musical Sleeping Bags Game

Set down one sleeping bag for every player except one. For example, if there are six players, set out only five sleeping bags. Place the sleeping bags in a circle with the openings facing in. Choose a leader to play the music. Before beginning, ask the players to stand at the outside ends of the sleeping bags. The leader starts the music, and the players walk in a circle around the sleeping bags. After a moment, the leader surprises the players by turning off the music! This is a signal to the players to quickly find a sleeping bag and lie down in it! The player left without a sleeping bag is eliminated from the game. Then one sleeping bag is removed. A player and a sleeping bag are removed with each round until two players and one bag are left. The player to lay down in the last sleeping bag is the winner.

Play Charades

Write the following words on separate pieces of paper: *happy, sad, angry, scared, surprised, car, bicycle, truck, bus, house, dog, cat, mouse, snake, man, woman,* and *baby.* Fold them over and put them in a hat. Each player gets a turn at choosing a word to act out without speaking. If you think you know what the word is, shout it out. (Do not return that word to the hat.) The person who guesses correctly now gets to act out a word.

Barbie Party Hint: Create a cozy corner in your party room filled with all your stuffed animals and pillows from around the house. This will be a nice place for your friends to sit and chat.

Bead-It Activity

For this fun activity, make sure to have plenty of beads, fishing wire, and clasps. Divide the beads into several empty egg cartons so your guests won't have to reach across the table, and have two guests share a carton. Write down all of your guests' names on small pieces of paper—don't forget to write down your name, too. Put the names into a hat. Let everyone pick out someone else's name. Gather around a table and start beading necklaces, earrings, and bracelets for the friends whose names were picked. If there is an uneven number of people, then you, Host of the Party, get to pick two names!

Barbie Party Hint: Make cleanup easy—use paper tablecloths, cups, and plates.

Nighttime Fun

Sleepovers are a great time to watch movies. Rent some of your favorite videos and enjoy them with your friends. Some suggestions:
• *The Princess Bride*
• *The Wizard of Oz*
• *Willy Wonka and the Chocolate Factory*
• *Home Alone*
• *The Indian in the Cupboard*
• *The Little Mermaid*

ⓅPajamas and Pizza: The Ultimate Combo!

Pizza is always fun and delicious to eat, but it tastes even better when you're eating it while wearing pj's! Have some delivered or, better yet, make pizza from scratch with your guests. Cooking with friends is always fun!

Make Your Own Pizzas!
The following makes about two 8-inch pizzas:
- 2 1/2 cups all-purpose flour
- 1 teaspoon salt
- 1 envelope dried yeast
- 2 tablespoons olive oil
- 1 cup hot water
- 2 tablespoons tomato paste
- shredded mozzarella cheese
- 1 bell pepper, chopped
- 1 small onion, chopped

Mix the flour and salt together. Add the yeast, oil, and hot water. Mix into dough with your hands. On a floured work surface, knead the dough for about 5 minutes (or until it is shiny and plastic looking). Put the dough into a large bowl, cover it with a clean dish towel, and let it rise in a warm, draft-free place for one hour. After an hour, preheat the oven to 350° F. Roll the dough into two balls and flatten them with a rolling pin into a circle about 8 inches wide. Place them on a cookie sheet. Spread on some tomato paste, and add mozzarella cheese, veggies, and anything else that would taste delicious on homemade pizza. Sprinkle olive oil on the top and bake it in the oven for 15–20 minutes.

> While the pizza dough is rising, play a couple of rounds of musical sleeping bags and charades.

> Not into making your own dough? Try using pita, French bread, or even bagels to create individual pizzas instead!

Super Sleepover Menu
Evening:
Potato Chips
Pizza
S'mores
Fruit Slushes
Morning:
Pancake Sundaes
Cereal
Juice

S'mores

For about 18 s'mores, you'll need:
- 1 jar marshmallow fluff (room temperature)
- 1 box graham crackers
- 1 bag mini-chocolate bars (room temperature)

Spread some marshmallow fluff on a graham cracker. (Don't push down too hard—graham crackers love to crumble!) Place a chocolate bar on top of the marshmallow fluff and top with another graham cracker. *Voilà!* A yummy sandwich!

Fruit Slushes

To make 4 glasses of slush, you'll need:
- 12 ounces orange juice
- 12 ounces pineapple juice
- 12 ounces cranberry juice

Pour the different juices into three separate ice trays and freeze until you have frozen juice cubes. Fill a blender 3/4 of the way with one color of cubes. Blend them until they become a slush. Put the mixture aside in a bowl. Do the same with the other two flavors of juice, keeping the mixtures separate. Then, using a ladle, scoop each layer of different-colored juice slush into tall glasses for a yummy, multi-layered, colorful drink!

Good Morning, Sunshine

Since you'll probably be up most of the night chatting and telling ghost stories, you'll want to serve up a really hearty breakfast so your pals will feel energized when they leave your house. Try making some pancake sundaes. And it's always good to have cereal, bagels, or muffins on hand, too!

Pancake Sundaes

For 8–12 pancakes, you'll need:
- 1 egg
- 1 cup all-purpose flour, sifted
- 3/4 cup milk
- 1 tablespoon sugar
- 2 tablespoons vegetable oil
- 3 teaspoons baking powder
- 1/2 teaspoon salt

Beat the egg until fluffy. Add the rest of the ingredients and mix until smooth. Have an adult grease a hot skillet and drop a serving spoonful onto the skillet—one spoonful for each pancake. When each bubbles and the edges are brown, turn over just once.

Toppings for 8–12 pancakes:
- 3 bananas, split in half and quartered
- 1 large carton strawberry yogurt
- 1 large carton vanilla yogurt

To serve, place one or two pancakes on a plate. Top each pancake with two banana pieces and one scoop each of the strawberry and vanilla yogurt. Enjoy!

Bed Head Party Favors

To help with morning hair, pass out scrunchies, barrettes, and headbands. Then have everyone put their hair into high pigtails or mini-ponies. For mini-ponies, make at least five mini-pigtails out of small sections of hair all over your head. Let everyone keep the beaded jewelry and hair accessories as party favors!

Star-Spangled Summer Celebration Party

For this star-spangled, patriotic, summer holiday celebration, hang up red, white, and blue streamers and balloons in your party room or backyard.

Barbie Party Hint: Atmosphere is important—don't forget to play your favorite music!

You're invited to a
July 4th Star-Spangled Celebration*

Where: Jessica's house
123 Kansas Ave.

When: July 4, 11:30 a.m.

RSVP: (880) 555-1212

*Be Patriotic: Wear red, white, and blue!

All American Fun
Organize some really fun, old-fashioned American games such as a scavenger hunt, a three-legged race, an egg toss, and a Jell-O eating contest.

Three-Legged Race Game
Each player needs a partner. Designate a starting line and a finish line. The partners stand behind the starting line side-by-side, with their inside legs loosely tied together with a rag or a scarf. At the signal to start, the partners hobble off toward the finish line. If the partners fall, they get up as quickly as possible and continue toward the finish line. This race should be played on grass since most partners fall at least once. The first team to cross the finish line and return to the start wins a prize.

Scavenger Hunt Game

A scavenger hunt can be inside, outside, or both! The day before your guests arrive, make a list of objects for them to find. (Remember that you will need to make or buy multiples of each item for each team to find.) If the game is played inside, make sure to hide the items on the list only in the room or rooms you want your guests to "hunt" in. Give your friends copies of the list and bags for collecting the items. Then let the hunt begin! The player or team to find the most objects after 30 minutes wins.

Scavenger Hunt Item Ideas: small rock, paper clip, pencil, pink socks, Barbie accessories.

Egg Toss Game

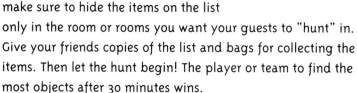

Make sure to play this outside or you'll get eggs all over your home! And warn players beforehand that this can get messy! Divide the players into pairs and have each person face their teammate about three feet apart. One player in each team holds an egg. At the signal to start, the players with the eggs carefully toss them to their partners. Those who catch the eggs take one step back and toss the egg back to their partner. With each successful throw, the distance between the partners is made wider. The last team to complete a toss without breaking their egg is the winner! (Tell your guests to remove bracelets, watches, or rings to avoid eggs coming in contact with them and breaking!)

Jell-O Eating Contest

Have the players sit around a table with their hands clasped behind their necks. Place a bowl of Jell-O in front of each contestant. When the "Start" command is given all the players should begin eating. The first one to completely eat all the Jell-O in their bowl is the winner. This is a messy activity, so be sure to cover the table with a tablecloth—and provide the players with napkins to protect their clothes!

**Star-Spangled
Celebration Menu**
Potato Chips
Pretzels
Hamburgers and Buns
Hot Dogs and Buns
Ketchup
Mustard
Corn on the Cob
Barbie's Brownies
Lemonade Fizz

Food, Glorious Food!

Serve your favorites like hot dogs,
hamburgers, and corn on the cob.
And brownies will make a big hit
with your guests, especially when these
chocolatey delights are washed down with
some Lemonade Fizz (add some seltzer
water to the lemonade to get that fizz
that tickles the roof of your mouth).

Corn on the Cob

- 1 ear of corn per person
- butter
- salt and pepper

Husk the corn, making sure to remove
all the silky threads. Dip it into cold
water to wash off all the bits of thread.
Then wrap each ear tightly in aluminum
foil. Turning it frequently, grill on the
barbecue for about 10 minutes. Serve with
butter, salt, and pepper. (Corn on the cob
can also be boiled in a large pot, without
the aluminum foil, for 10–15 minutes
until soft.)

Barbie's Brownies

To make about 12 brownies you'll need:

- 1/2 cup all-purpose flour, sifted
- 1/2 cup unsweetened baking cocoa
- 1/4 teaspoon salt
- 3 large eggs
- 3/4 cup granulated sugar
- 6 tablespoons applesauce
- 2 tablespoons vegetable oil
- 1 teaspoon vanilla extract
- vegetable cooking spray

Preheat oven to 350° F. Spray an 8-inch square baking pan with vegetable cooking spray and set aside. In a medium-sized bowl, combine the flour, cocoa, and salt. Mix well. In a large bowl, whisk together the eggs, sugar, applesauce, oil, and vanilla. Next, stir in the flour mixture until the lumps are gone. Pour batter into the prepared 8-inch pan. Bake until a toothpick inserted into the center comes out clean—about 25 minutes. Ask an adult to remove the pan from the oven and place it on a wire rack. Let it cool for 15–20 minutes before cutting it into squares.

Barbie's Extra-Fudge Brownie Secret: Stir a half bag of semisweet chocolate chips into the mixture before putting it all into the pan!

Vicki

Star-Studded Party Favors

Decorate brown paper bags with each guest's name written in a star. Fill the bags with star stickers, a few postage stamps, and stationery. Tie up the bags with red, white, or blue ribbons.

Pretty in Pink Tea Party

Tell Your Pals

Ask all your friends to wear pink and to bring along their Barbie dolls and clothing accessories to this very special tea party. Also, remind them to bring along a plain white T-shirt for batiking.

Barbie Party Hint:
Set the table and put the food out about an hour before your guests arrive.

P Crayon Batik T-shirt Activity

In case some of your guests forget to bring T-shirts, have some extras on hand. Materials needed for each person:
- white cotton T-shirt
- crayons
- paper towels
- one iron and ironing board to share

Using the crayons, press down hard and draw any kind of design onto the T-shirt. Dampen a few layers of paper towels and lay the cotton T-shirt between the paper towels. Next, with an adult's help, press the paper towels dry with an iron set on low (no steam) to melt the crayons. The results look super!

Dress-up Time

You and your friends lay out all of your Barbie outfits on the floor. Put out a box full of silly hats, feather boas, and some costume jewelry so you can all play dress-up, too! Hold a contest to see whose Barbie doll and which friend look best in their outfits. Make up different categories such as Cutest First Day of School Outfit, Silliest Evening Wear, and Most Glam Outfit.

Pretty in Pink Menu
Finger Sandwiches (cream cheese, peanut butter, egg salad)
Chocolate Chip Cookies
Barbie Skirt Cake
Peppermint Ice Cream Soda
Herbal Sun Tea

Finger Foods and Barbie Skirt Cake

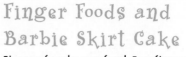

Finger foods are fun! For finger sandwiches, try mini bagels with cream cheese or peanut butter. Or use sandwich bread, remove the crust, and cut the sandwiches into different shapes. For dessert serve some Barbie Cake. All you need to do is buy or make some angel food cake in a bundt pan. Decorate the cake with pink frosting to make it look like the bottom of a dress. Then, place your Barbie doll on a stand in the center of the cake to make it look as if she is wearing a cake "skirt."

Peppermint Ice Cream Soda

For each soda, you'll need:
• 1 cup milk
• 1 cup seltzer
• 2 scoops peppermint ice cream

Mix the milk and seltzer water together; add the ice cream and serve.

Herbal Sun Tea

You can use the sun to brew some great tea! Get a big glass jar at least a foot tall. Fill it with cold water. Put in 7 herbal tea bags. If you like it sweet, add two teaspoons of sugar per tea bag. Cover with a piece of aluminum foil and tighten to seal. Place in the sun, away from where people might walk and knock it over. Three hours later, you'll have delicious sun-brewed tea!

Party Favors

Decorate bags with pink and gold glitter paint. Let dry. Fill them up with some pink peppermint candy and various herbal tea bags. Include your favorite handwritten recipe. Remember, party favors don't have to be expensive to be great! Your friends will appreciate something that you made for them yourself.

Monster Madness Halloween Party

Where:
Judy's house
2031 Maple Ave.

When:
Oct. 31, 5:30 p.m.

RSVP:
(880) 555-1212

Come in costume!

A Halloween Costume Party!

Spooky Invitations

Halloween is a great time to gather together friends for a party that's sure to be a blast! Create your own invitations that are in the shape of a witch's hat. Make sure to tell everyone to wear their best costume.

Barbie Party Hint:
Be a gracious hostess and introduce everyone to each other.

Creepy Decorations

Set up your party room like a creepy haunted house. Hang scary Halloween decorations such as fake spiderwebs, paper moons and stars, paper skeletons, and rubber bats from the ceiling. Keep the lights dimmed and play spooky music.

Let's Play Games

What would a Halloween party be without Pumpkin Decorating or Bobbing for Apples? Or try something different and have a crafts table set out so friends can make their own masks.

The Ghost Game

As an icebreaker, have your friends sit in a circle and play a couple of rounds of Ghost. The purpose of Ghost is to add letters together to make *someone else* spell a real five-letter word without spelling a word yourself. Keep a dictionary nearby so you can check a word if someone challenges it. Have all your guests sit in a circle. You start by calling out a letter of the alphabet. The person next in the circle clockwise calls out another letter, and so on. The first person to spell an actual word gets a G. Then he or she starts the game again. The last player to get all the letters for the word G-H-O-S-T wins. (Players must work toward spelling real words, adding letters in an order that makes sense.)

A-D-O-R-
A-C-A-T

Edible Jewelry Activity

Fill plastic containers with skinny licorice ropes and any candies and cereals that have center holes. Make a knot in one end of the licorice and string the candies and cereal, one at a time, to make a bracelet or a necklace. Wear your jewelry—or eat it!

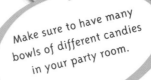

Make sure to have many bowls of different candies in your party room.

Monster Madness
Halloween Party

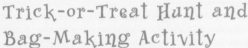

Trick-or-Treat Hunt and Bag-Making Activity

Before you start, provide each of your guests with a paper bag, crayons, markers, glue, scissors, and colored construction paper to decorate their own trick-or-treat bags. Your trick-or-treat candy hunt can be either inside or outside. The day of your party, hide wrapped candy only in the rooms or places you want your guests to "hunt." The player or team to fill their bag with the most candy after 15 minutes wins.

Halloween Twist Game

Before the day of your Halloween bash, ask your parents for an old white sheet that you can use. Make sure to tell them that it will be ruined! Then use crayons to draw different-colored circles, the size of a large plate, about a foot apart on the sheet. Have your parents help you tack the sheet down onto the carpet. Then invite your friends to play Halloween Twist. Each person stands with each foot in a circle. Make sure the players remove their shoes. You turn on the music. When you switch it off, they have to find two circles for their hands. Then you turn on the music again. When you switch it off, they have to move their *feet* to two different circles, without moving their hands. Keep alternating hands and feet and see what happens!

Monster Madness Menu
Lots of Candy
Trick or Treat Munchies
Assorted Sandwiches (ham,
tuna, chicken salad, and cheese)
Bean, Onion, or Salsa Dip
Potato or Tortilla Chips
Cut-up Veggies to Dip
Creepy Cookies
Juice

Trick-or-Treat Munchies
Celebrate your Halloween party with
tricky treats! Serve up some Pumpkin
Surprises: pumpkin-faced oranges cut
in half with the insides scooped out and
filled with ice cream or frozen yogurt.
Or how about a bucket of Creepy Crawler
Creations (gummy worms trapped inside
chocolate pudding). Yucky to look at,
but yummy to eat!

Creepy Cookies
Follow the Sugar Cookie recipe on page 11.
But this time, add orange food coloring into
the mix and then use creature-shaped cookie
cutters. Decorate with black frosting for a
spooky good treat!

It's Been a Gobbly Good Time!
As a parting gift for your friends,
fill up a plastic bag with some
special candy and throw in some
funky, spooky Halloween stickers.

27

Happy Holidays Party

Seasonal Invites

Make your own invitations to this winter holiday party in the shape of a snowflake. And for some extra added fun, fill the envelopes with lots of multicolored homemade confetti!

It's a Holiday Party!

Where: Kelly's house
333 Rochester Ave.

When: Dec. 24, 5:30 p.m.

RSVP by December 18
(880) 555-1212

Barbie Party Hint:
Try to plan your party about six weeks in advance. This will give you lots of time to make sure everything is absolutely perfect!

Make sure to get holiday invitations out early, before your friends are all booked up!

Happy Holidays Decorations

Dress up the party room for winter. Spray fake snow on window ledges. Cut out snowflakes and hang them on the walls and windows. Fill up the room with gold and silver noisemakers, balloons, confetti, and party hats.

Happy Holidays Musical Chairs Game

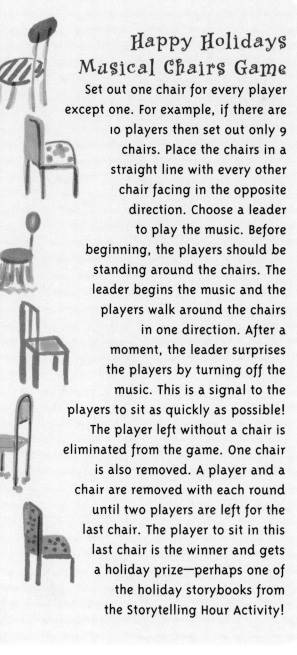

Set out one chair for every player except one. For example, if there are 10 players then set out only 9 chairs. Place the chairs in a straight line with every other chair facing in the opposite direction. Choose a leader to play the music. Before beginning, the players should be standing around the chairs. The leader begins the music and the players walk around the chairs in one direction. After a moment, the leader surprises the players by turning off the music. This is a signal to the players to sit as quickly as possible! The player left without a chair is eliminated from the game. One chair is also removed. A player and a chair are removed with each round until two players are left for the last chair. The player to sit in this last chair is the winner and gets a holiday prize—perhaps one of the holiday storybooks from the Storytelling Hour Activity!

Cool Calendars Activity

Have everything you and your guests will need to make your own calendars. Set out 12 sheets of colored construction paper per guest and plenty of rulers, markers, crayons, and scissors. Be creative with your calendars and decorate them with beads, buttons, and stickers. When you're all done, write down each other's birthdays and other fun and special holidays, so you'll remember them in the New Year!

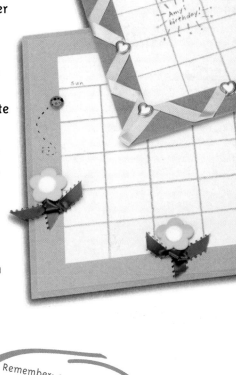

Remember: 30 days hath September, April, June, and November! All the rest have 31, except for February which has 28, and 29 in each leap year!

Storytelling Hour Activity

Christmas, Hanukkah, Kwanzaa—all are fun, traditional holidays, celebrated by different peoples all over the world. Each holiday has its own special history and stories. Find at least one storybook for each holiday and share it wth your guests. A good time for storytelling is when your guests are eating or involved in a craft activity.

Hunting for Stars Game

You will need at least six packets of stars, each packet a different color. (If you want, you can cut out paper stars yourself. Plan on at least five pairs per guest.) Before your guests arrive, hide the stars around the party room. The person who collects the most pairs of matching stars—stars of the same color—wins a prize.

⚠P Make Your Own Holiday Mask

Materials needed for each guest:
- a paper plate
- 2 feet of string
- markers
- crayons
- scissors

Cut a hole in the middle of your plate and poke your nose through. Feel where your eyes and mouth are by pressing lightly and mark the spot gently with a crayon. Then cut out the eye holes. Decorate your plate mask any way you like. Fasten string to each side and tie behind your head!

Yammy Munchies

Serve up some hot cocoa and eggnog. For party munchies, mix up a big bowl with pretzels, roasted peanuts, white chocolates, and your favorite crunchy cereal. Mmmmm! Another great food to serve at your party is chicken wings.

Gingerbread Cookies

For 12–18 cookies, you'll need:
- 3 cups all-purpose flour
- 1 teaspoon baking soda
- 1 tablespoon ground ginger
- 1/2 cup butter
- 1 cup dark brown sugar, packed
- 1 egg
- 4 tablespoons light corn syrup
- cookie cutters

Preheat oven to 350° F. Mix the flour, baking soda, and ginger in a bowl. Mix in butter till mixture resembles fine bread crumbs. Beat egg and corn syrup together in a separate bowl, then add to flour mixture and mix until it forms a ball. Knead on floured work space. Refrigerate for one hour. Roll out to 1/2 inch thickness and cut into shapes with cookie cutters. Bake for 10–15 minutes until crispy. Have an adult take the tray out of the oven with oven mitts and allow to cool for 1/2 hour before removing cookies from tray.

Holiday Cookie-Decorating Activity

Using the gingerbread cookies or white sugar cookies, plan a cookie-decorating activity. Have plenty of tubes of different-colored frosting, jimmies, small chocolate candies, colored sugar crystals, and sprinkles. Use the frosting first as "glue," and then decorate your cookies to look like animals, people, or anything else your heart desires.

Sock It to Them Party Favors

For a different kind of party favor use socks (new ones, please!). Fill up each sock with lots of candy and include a homemade personal holiday card for each of your friends. Tie them up with colored ribbon or yarn. Your friends will feel special because you took the time to tell them how much you care!

Hello again!

Now that you've been through an entire year of parties, see if you can make up some of your own party themes! Mix and match activities and games, recipes and party favors, and invent a reason to have your friends come by and hang out!

Hope you have fun! See you at your next Barbie bash!

Love,

Barbie